Hell Island

Hell Island by Matthew Reilly was originally commissioned and published for the 2005 Books Alive campaign in Australia. Books Alive is an Australian Government initiative developed through the Australia Council for the Arts.

Australian Government

Australia **Council**
for the Arts

BOOKS ALIVE

Also by Matthew Reilly

Contest
Ice Station
Temple
Area 7
Scarecrow
Hover Car Racer
Seven Ancient Wonders
The Six Sacred Stones

Hell Island

Matthew Reilly

First published 2005 by Books Alive, an Australian Government
initiative developed through the Australia Council for the Arts.

This edition published 2006 in association with World Book Day
'Quick Reads' by Pan Books, an imprint of Pan Macmillan,
a division of Macmillan Publishers Limited
Pan Macmillan, 20 New Wharf Road, London N1 9RR
Basingstoke and Oxford
Associated companies throughout the world
www.panmacmillan.com

ISBN 978-0-330-44232-9

10

A CIP catalogue record for this book is available from
the British Library

Typeset by SX Composing DTP, Rayleigh, Essex
Printed and bound in Great Britain by
CPI Group (UK) Ltd, Croydon, CR0 4YY

Distributed By:
Grass Roots Press
Toll Free: 1-888-303-3213
Fax: (780) 413-6582
Web Site: www.grassrootsbooks.net

PROLOGUE

THE LAST MAN STANDING

TERRIFIED, WOUNDED AND OUT of ammo, Lieutenant Rick 'Razor' Haynes staggered down the aircraft carrier's tight passage. Blood poured from a gunshot wound to his left thigh. His face was badly scratched.

He panted, gasping for breath. He was the last one left, the last member of his entire Marine force still alive.

He could hear the enemy behind him.

Grunting, growling.

Stalking him, hunting him down.

The enemy *knew* they had him; knew he was out of ammunition, out of contact with base and out of comrades in arms.

The passageway was hardly wide enough for his shoulders. Situated one level below the flight deck, it gave access to the senior officers' quarters on this aircraft carrier. It had grey steel

1

walls studded with rivets – the kind you find on a warship.

In agony, Haynes arrived at a thick steel door leading from the passage and tumbled through it, landing in a room. He reached up and pulled the heavy steel door shut behind him and locked it.

A second later, the great steel door shuddered violently, pounded from the other side.

His face covered in sweat, Haynes breathed deeply, glad of the brief rest.

He was still shocked from seeing what the enemy force had done to his teammates.

No soldier deserved to die in such a gruesome manner. It was beyond ruthless what they'd done to his men.

Yet the way they had overcome his force of 600 United States Marines had been brilliant.

At one point during his escape from the upper deck of the ship, Haynes had figured he would end his own life before they caught him. Now, without any bullets, he couldn't even do that.

A grunt disturbed him.

It seemed to come from the darkness on the far side of the room.

Haynes looked up just as a shape came rushing out of the darkness. It was dark, hairy and man-sized. And it was screaming like a chimpanzee gone insane. Only this was no chimpanzee.

It slammed into Haynes, ramming him back against the door. His head hit the steel door hard. The blow stunned him but did not knock him out.

As he slumped to the floor he saw the creature pull out a shiny, long-bladed knife. Haynes wished it *had* knocked him out, because then he wouldn't have to know what it did to him next . . .

The death scream of Razor Haynes rang out from the aircraft carrier.

It would not be heard by a single friendly soul.

For this carrier was 1,000 miles from anywhere. It was docked at an island that lay 500 miles from its nearest neighbour.

It had once been known as Grant Island, but strangely it no longer appeared on any maps. It had been used in the Second World War by the Japanese as an airfield.

In 1943, after extremely bloody fighting, it had been captured by the American Marines from the Japanese. Because the fighting had been so fierce, the Marines had given it a nickname.

They'd called it Hell Island.

FIRST ASSAULT

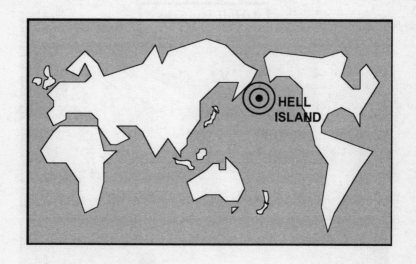

HELL ISLAND

1500 HOURS

1 AUGUST 2005

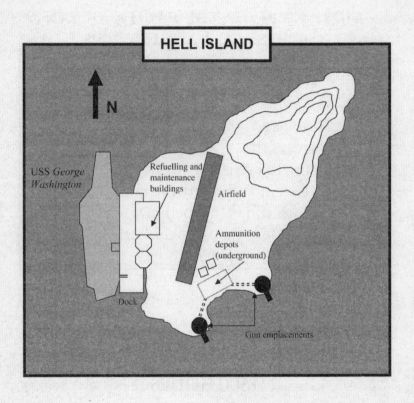

HELL ISLAND

N

USS *George Washington*

Refuelling and maintenance buildings

Airfield

Ammunition depots (underground)

Dock

Gun emplacements

AIRSPACE OVER THE PACIFIC OCEAN
1500 HOURS, 1 AUGUST 2005

THE AIRCRAFT SHOT ACROSS the sky at near supersonic speed.

It was a cargo plane, used to transport US special forces units.

According to current maps it was flying over empty ocean. But suddenly the ramp at the rear of the plane rumbled open. Dozens of men jumped off it into the sky behind the plane.

The group of forty paratroopers fell to earth. They wore high-altitude jumpsuits – full-face breathing masks and black bodysuits. They angled their bodies down as they fell, pointing into the wind like human spears.

It was a classic high-altitude, low-opening (HALO) drop. You jumped from 37,000 feet, and fell fast and hard. Then you opened your parachute dangerously close to the ground, right at your drop zone.

The strange thing about these paratroopers

was that they were clearly falling in four separate groups. That's because they were actually separate teams.

Crack teams. The best of the best from every corner of the US armed forces.

One unit from the 82nd Airborne Division, brilliant attack troops.

One team of elite Navy SEALs, the best assassins in the world.

One Delta team, always very secretive.

And last of all, one team of force reconnaissance Marines, the very best Marines in the Corps.

They fell like bullets into a thick band of cloud.

After nearly a full minute they came through the cloud into the middle of a massive ocean storm. The rain pounded their facemasks. In the ocean beneath the dark clouds, giant waves rolled and crashed.

Through the rain, their target came into view. It was the tiny island that did not appear on maps any more, an island with an aircraft carrier parked alongside it.

It was Hell.

*

Leading the Marine team was Captain Shane M. Schofield, nicknamed 'Scarecrow'.

Behind his mask, Schofield had a rugged face, black hair and blue eyes. Slicing down across those eyes were two ugly scars, one for each eye. The scars were wounds from a mission that had gone wrong. They were also the reason for his nickname. Once on the ground he'd hide those eyes behind a pair of silver reflecting sunglasses – the kind that wrapped around.

Schofield was a quiet and thoughtful man who had a special reputation in the Marine Corps because of the special missions he had been involved in. The Marine Corps (like any group of human beings) is filled with gossip and rumour. Someone always knew someone who had been there, or who had seen the medical report, or who had cleaned up the mess afterwards. There were many rumours about Schofield and some of them were simply too outrageous to be true.

One: he had been involved in a huge multi-force battle in Antarctica. It had been a bloody and brutal struggle with two of America's allies, France and Britain.

Two: he'd saved the American president's life

9

when there had been an attempted military coup. It was said that during the fighting the Scarecrow (a former pilot) had actually flown a space shuttle, destroyed it, and then come *back* and rescued the president from certain death.

Of course, nobody could say if this were true. Even so it didn't stop Schofield's new unit talking about it.

One thing about Shane Schofield *was* known to be true: this was his first mission after four months on stress leave. On this occasion someone really *had* seen the medical report, and now all his men on this mission knew about it.

They also knew the cause of his stress.

During his last mission, Schofield's ability to cope had been tested to the limit. Loved ones close to him had been captured and killed. It was even said that at one point on that mission he had tried to kill himself.

All of which meant that the other members of his team were slightly less than confident in their leader.

Was he up to this mission? Was he a time-bomb waiting to explode? Was he a basket case who would lose it at the first sign of trouble?

They were about to find out.

As he shot downward through the sky, Schofield thought about their mission briefing earlier that day.

Their target was Hell Island.

Actually, the target was the ageing aircraft carrier parked at Hell Island, the USS *George Washington*.

The *George Washington* had been heading home on its last official journey. It was going to be decommissioned. Because of this, it only had a skeleton crew aboard and was accompanied by only two escort boats.

But soon after the *George Washington* had arrived at the isolated island to pick up some special cargo, a fierce tsunami had struck from the north.

All contact with the ship, its two escorts and the island's communications centre had been lost.

However, a North Korean nuclear submarine had been spotted in the area a day earlier, coming out of the Bering Sea. Its position was unknown, but its presence was suspicious.

What were the North Koreans doing in the area? What did they want with the *George Washington*?

Schofield and the other teams were being sent in to find out what was going on and report back. Schofield was very troubled by something other than the mission: why were there other special forces units on this mission? Why were the Marines here with the 82nd, the SEALS and Delta?

Normally you never mixed and matched special forces units. They all had different approaches to mission situations, and could easily trip over each other. It just wasn't done.

To Schofield this smelled a lot like an exercise.

Except for one thing.

They were all carrying live ammo.

The Pacific Ocean stretched away below them in every direction. Somewhere in the middle of it all was the small dot of land known as Hell Island.

The *George Washington* lay at the western end of Hell Island. On the island itself, not far from the carrier, were some big gun positions facing south and east. At the north-eastern tip of the island was a hill that looked like a small volcano.

A voice came through Schofield's earpiece. *'All team leaders, this is Delta Six. We're going for the eastern end of the island and we'll work our way back to the boat. Your target is the flight deck: Airborne, the bow; SEALs, mid-section; Marines, aft.'*

Just like we were told in the briefing, Schofield thought.

This was typical of Delta. They were great soldiers but, boy, were they born show-offs. No matter who they were working with, they always acted like they were in charge. That was true today, even though they were working with three of the best special forces units in the world.

'Roger that, Delta Leader,' came the SEAL leader's voice.

'Copy, Delta Six,' came the Airborne response.

Schofield didn't reply.

The Delta leader said, *'Marine Six? Scarecrow? You copy?'*

Schofield sighed. 'I was at the mission briefing, too, Delta Six. And, last I noticed, I don't have any short-term memory problems. I know the mission plan.'

'Cut the attitude, Scarecrow,' the Delta leader said. His name was Hugh Gordon, so naturally his call-sign was 'Flash'. *'We're all on the same team here.'*

'What? *Your* team?' Schofield said. 'How about this: how about you don't break radio silence until you've got something important to say? Scarecrow, out.'

Schofield wasn't just being difficult when he told the Delta leader to keep quiet. It was more important than that. Even a coded radio signal could be caught these days so, if you transmitted, you had to assume someone was listening.

And they probably were. France, Syria, Iran and North Korea, countries not known for their friendship towards America, had built new radio decoders. These were designed to pin-point the location of a particular type of American military radio. And guess what? Schofield and the other teams were using these particular radios on this mission.

Schofield switched to his team's private channel. 'Marines. Switch off your radios.

Listening mode only. Go to short-wave UHF channel if you want to talk to me.'

A few of his Marines thought about it before obeying, but obey they did. They flicked off their radios.

The four groups of parachutists fell towards the deck of the *George Washington*. A thousand feet above it, they pulled on their ripcords and their chutes opened. Now their falls slowed and they floated toward the carrier. While the other three teams touched down lightly on the flight deck of the giant ship, the Delta team landed on the eastern side of the island. It was a perfect landing with all of them arriving in their assigned positions, guns up.

They had just arrived in Hell.

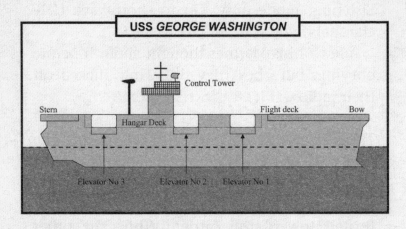

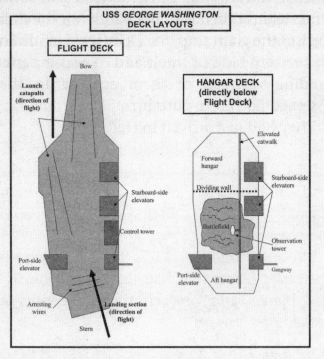

FLIGHT DECK, USS *GEORGE WASHINGTON*

Rain pounded down on the flight deck.

As Schofield's team landed one after the other, they unclipped their huge nylon chutes before these fell to the ground. The wind was so strong that it blew the chutes away, leaving the ten Marines standing in the pouring rain on the flight deck holding their MP-7 machine guns pointed outwards.

One after the other, they ripped off their face-masks, and scanned the deck carefully.

Schofield took off his facemask, too, and put on his signature silver sunglasses, masking his eyes. He took a good look at the deck around them. It looked like a giant runway, built on top of the warship.

The entire flight deck was deserted, except for the other teams that had just landed on it. A few planes and one chunky helicopter sat parked on runways.

There were star-shaped splatters of blood everywhere, but there were no bodies. Not one.

'Mother,' Schofield said to his number two, 'what do you think?'

Gena Newman was her real name, gunnery sergeant was her rank, but 'Mother' was her nickname and it didn't have anything to do with being a warm, cosy mother figure. In fact it was short for a slightly longer word starting with 'Mother . . .'.

At six feet two, 200 pounds, and with a fully shaven head, Mother cut a mean figure. Tough, no-nonsense and fiercely loyal, she had been with Schofield on many missions, including the bad ones. She was reckoned to be the best shot in the Corps. Once she had been offered her pick of missions *outside* Schofield's command. She'd looked the commandant of the Marine Corps in the eye and said, 'I'm staying with the Scarecrow, sir.'

'What do I think?' Mother replied. 'I think this is seriously fucked up. I was planning on spending this weekend watching David Hasselhoff DVDs. No one takes me away from the Hoff.'

She gazed at the blood splatters on a nearby

plane. 'No, this was way suspect from the start. I mean, why are we here with the other troops? I'd rather just work with swordsmen.'

Swordsman was her word for a Marine: a reference to the swords they wore with their full dress uniforms.

'Marines,' Schofield called, 'the control tower. Let's move.'

Since they'd been assigned the aft end of the ship, Schofield's Marines had the task of investigating the carrier's six-storey-high control tower.

They moved quickly through the rain and crossed the wide flight deck. When they arrived at the base of the tower they found the main door covered in blood with about a million bullet holes in it. The door's hinges were blasted to hell.

Looking up, Schofield saw that every single antenna and piece of radar equipment on top of the control tower had been broken or destroyed. The main antenna mast was broken in the middle and lay tilted over, probably hit by a shoulder-launched rocket.

'What in God's name happened here?' one of Schofield's Marines asked softly. He was a big, broad guy, with a thick neck. His name: Corporal Harold 'Hulk' Hogan.

'More than a tsunami, that's for sure,' Sergeant Paulo 'Pancho' Sanchez said. Sanchez was older and more senior than Hulk, a sly, sarcastic type. 'Tsunamis don't shoot you in the head.'

The voice of the SEAL leader came through their headsets: *'All units, this is Gator. Starboard elevator one has been disabled. We're taking the stairs, heading for the main hangar bay below the flight deck.'*

'This is Condor,' the Airborne leader called in. *'I got evidence of a firefight by the missile launcher up at the bow. Hell of a lot of blood, but not a single body.'*

'Delta Six here. We're on the island proper. No sign of anything yet.'

Schofield didn't send out any report.

'Sir,' Sanchez said to him, 'you gonna call in?'

'No.'

Sanchez threw a quick look toward the Marine next to him, a tall guy named Bigfoot. Sanchez was one of the men who'd been unsure about Schofield's mental state and his ability to lead this mission.

'Not even to tell the others where we are?' Sanchez said.

'No.'

'But what about—'

'Sergeant,' Schofield said sharply, 'did you ask your last commander to explain everything to you?'

'No, sir.'

'So don't start doing it now. Focus on the mission in hand, please.'

Sanchez bit his lip and nodded. 'Yes, sir.'

'Now, if no one else has anything to say, let's see what's going on in this tower. Move.'

They jumped over the twisted steel door and charged into the darkness of the aircraft carrier's central tower.

THE TOWER, USS *GEORGE WASHINGTON*

They moved quickly up a series of tight ladders that formed the spine of the control tower. There was blood on the rungs. But still no bodies.

They came to the middle floor of the tower –

the lookout level. It consisted of three huge windows, giving them a full view of the flight deck below. There must have been fierce fighting in here, as the glass had either been cracked or completely smashed by gunfire. Blood smeared the glass and thousands of rounds of ammunition lay on the floor.

There were also a few guns lying about. These were mainly M-16s, but there were also a few M-4 Colt Commandos there too. The M-4 was a short-barrelled gun used by special forces teams worldwide.

Mother led a few of the marines up the last flight of stairs to the flight-control room. She returned a few minutes later.

'Same deal,' she reported. 'Bucketloads of blood, no bodies. All the windows smashed, and lots of spent ammo left on the floor. A hell of a firefight took place here, Scarecrow.'

As Schofield was about to reply, something caught his eye. It was one of the rifles on the floor, one of the M-4s.

He picked it up and took a good look at it.

From a distance it looked like a regular M-4, but it wasn't. It seemed to have been changed slightly.

The gun's trigger-guard was different: it had been made longer as if to fit an index finger that was also longer.

'What the hell is that?' Hulk said. 'Some kind of super gun?'

'Scarecrow,' Mother said, coming over, 'most of these blood splatters are the result of bullet impacts. But some aren't. They're . . . well . . . thicker. More like arterial flow. As if some of the dead had entire *limbs* cut off.'

Schofield's earpiece squawked.

'All units, this is Gator. We've just arrived at the main hangar deck and holy shit, people, have we got something to show you. We aren't the first force to have got here. And the guys before us didn't do well at all. I have a visual on at least two hundred pairs of hands all stacked up in a neat pile down here.'

Sanchez whispered, 'Did he just say . . . ?'

Gator knew they wouldn't believe it. *'Yes, you heard me right. Hands. Human hands. Cut off and stacked in a great big heap. What in God's name have we walked into here?'*

While the rest of their team listened in horror to Gator's gruesome report, Schofield and Mother went up to the flight-control room. It had been pretty much wrecked, but not totally.

'Mother, do a power-grid check, all grids, all levels, even externals. I'm gonna look for Air Tasking Orders.'

Air Tasking Orders were the orders the ship received daily from Pacific Command at Pearl Harbor.

Mother sat down at a console which had somehow stayed undamaged. Meanwhile, Schofield went to the captain's desk and attached some plastic explosive to the captain's safe.

A muffled boom later and he had the *George Washington*'s last fourteen orders from Pacific Command.

It was mainly routine stuff as the *George Washington* made her way back from the Indian Ocean to Hawaii, dropping in at Singapore and the Philippines on the way.

Until ten days ago . . . when the *George Washington* was ordered to divert to the Japanese island of Okinawa and pick up three companies of US Marines there, a force of about 600 men.

She was to ferry the Marines – not special forces, just regular troops – across the northern

Pacific and drop them off at a place that was not named, but which Schofield knew was Hell Island.

After unloading the Marines, the ship was then told to:

PICK UP DARPA SCIENCE TEAM FROM
LOCATION:
KNOX, MALCOLM C.
PENNEBAKER, ZACHARY B.
JOHNSON, SIMON W.
HENDRICKS, JAMES F.
RYAN, HARPER R.
HOGAN, SHANE M.
LIEBMANN, BEN C.
PERSONNEL ARE ALL SECURITY CLEARED
TO 'TOP SECRET'. THEY WILL HAVE
CARGO WHICH IS NOT TO BE SEEN BY
CREW OF *GEORGE WASHINGTON*.

DARPA was the Defence Advanced Research Projects Agency. The people who worked there were genius-level scientists who made high-tech weapons for the US military. After inventing the Internet and stealth technology, the rumour was that DARPA had recently been at work on super-strong, ultra-light body armour. There was also talk of a weapon called a supernova, the most powerful nuke ever devised.

It was getting clearer. The *George Washington* had been sent to drop off a large force of Marines and also pick up some scientists who had been at work here.

This made it look even more like an exercise – Marines being unloaded on a secret island where DARPA scientists had been at work.

'Scarecrow,' Mother said from her console, 'I see power is being taken from the *George Washington*'s nuclear reactor. It is being drained away by something on the island. And all other systems on the boat have been shut down: lights, air-conditioning, everything. And another thing,' Mother said. 'I'm picking up a weird radio signal being sent inside the *George Washington*.'

'Why is it weird?' Schofield said.

'Because it's not a voice signal. It sounds like a digital signal, a bit like my old dial-up modem.'

Schofield thought about it all: a power drain going off the ship. Digital radio signals inside the ship. A secret DARPA presence. And a gruesome stack of severed hands down in the hangar deck.

This didn't make sense at all.

'Mother,' he said, 'you got an AXS on you?' An AXS was a portable unit that picked up radio transmissions, but which most often was used as a bug detector.

'Sure have.'

'Jamming capabilities?'

'Multi-channel and single channel,' she said.

'Good,' Schofield said. 'Tune it in to those beeps. Stay on them. And just be ready to jam them.'

Gator's voice continued to come over his earpiece. The SEAL leader was describing the scene in the hangar bay:

'. . . *looks like the entire hangar has been laid out for an exercise of some sort. It's like an indoor battlefield. I've got artificial trenches, some low terrain, even an observation tower set up inside the hangar. Moving toward the nearest trench now – hey, what was that? Holy—'*

Braaaaaaaack-braack-braaack!

Gunfire rang out.

It came from the SEALs and from an unknown enemy force. The SEALs' silenced guns made a chilling *slit-slit-slit-slit-slit-slit* sound when they fired. Their enemies' guns made a different noise altogether; the assault rifles made more of a clattering sound.

The SEALs starting shouting to each other: *'They're coming out of the nearest trench!'*

'What the fuck *is that . . .'*

'It looks like a goddamn go—'

Crack-splat. The speaker never finished his sentence. There was the sound of a bullet slamming into a man's skull.

Then Gator's voice: *'Fire! Open fire! Mow 'em down!'*

In response to his order, the level of SEAL gunfire increased. But the SEALs' voices became more desperate.

'Jesus, they just keep coming! There are too many of them!'

'Get back to the stairs! Get back to the—'

'Shit! There are more back there! They're cutting us off! They've got us surrounded!'

'Gator's down! Oh, fuck, ah—'

The speaker's voice was suddenly cut off by a grunting noise that sounded like it was eating his radio-mike. There were scuffling noises and then the man screamed with terror. He panted desperately, as if struggling with some great beast. Indeed, it sounded as if some kind of creature had run into him full tilt *and had started to eat his face.*

Then there was a gunshot and there were no more screams. Schofield couldn't tell if it was the man who had fired or the thing that had attacked him.

And suddenly it was over.

Silence on the airwaves.

In the control tower of the giant ship, the members of Schofield's team looked at each other.

Sanchez reached for the radio – only for Schofield to swat his hand away.

'I said no signals.'

Sanchez didn't look happy, but obeyed.

One of the other teams, however, came over the line. *'SEAL team, this is Condor. What's going on? Come in!'*

Schofield waited for a reply.

None came.

But then, after thirty seconds or so, another rough scuffling sound could be heard, someone – or something – grabbing one of the SEAL team's radio-mikes.

Then a terrifying sound shot through the radio: a horrific animal roar.

'*SEAL team, I repeat! This is Condor! Come in!*' the Airborne leader kept saying over the radio.

'Scarecrow!' Mother shouted. 'I've got something here.'

'What?' Schofield hurried over to her console.

'Those binary beeps just went off the charts. It's like a thousand fax machines all dialled up at once. There was a jump thirty seconds ago as well, just after Condor called the SEALs the first time.'

'Shit . . .' Schofield said. 'Quickly, Mother. Find the ship's dry-dock security systems. Switch on the motion sensors.'

Every American warship had standard security features for use when they were in dry-dock. These included infrared motion sensors placed throughout the ship's main corridors. Their purpose was to detect intruders who might enter the boat when it was deserted. The USS *George Washington* had that system.

Mother switched on the sensor system. An image of the *George Washington* appeared on a big glass screen in the centre of the control room. 'Holy shit!' Hulk said, seeing the screen.

'Mama mia . . .' Sanchez breathed.

A river of red dots was moving out from the main hangar bay, heading toward the bow of the carrier, where a far smaller cluster of ten dots stood still: Condor's Airborne team.

Each dot represented a figure moving past the infrared sensors. There were perhaps 400 dots on the screen right now moving towards the Airborne team. For Schofield, things were starting to make sense.

The binary beeps were the coded communications of his enemy, who obviously had radio tracers. Damn.

'*SEAL team! Come in!*' Condor said again over the airwaves.

The dots on the glass screen began to move faster.

'Christ. He's got to get off the air,' Schofield said. 'He's bringing them right to him.'

'We have to tell him, warn him . . .' Sanchez said.

'How?' Mother demanded. 'If we call him on our radios, we'll only be giving away our own position.'

'We can't just leave him there, with all those things on the way!'

'Wanna bet?' Mother said.

'The Airborne guys know their job,' Schofield said. 'So do we. And our job is not to babysit them. We have to trust they know what they're doing. We also have our own tasks to perform: to find out what's been going on here and to end it. Which is why we're going down to the main hangar right now.'

Schofield's team hustled out of the control tower and slid down the ladders.

Last to leave was Sanchez, covering the rear.

With a final glare at Schofield's departing back, he pulled out his radio, selected the Airborne team's private channel, and started talking.

Then he took off after the others.

Down through the tower, the Marines came to the flight deck, but instead of going outside, they kept going down below decks.

They walked through tight dark passageways, where blood smears lined the walls.

But still no bodies, no nothing.

Then over the main radio network came the sound of gunfire: Condor's Airborne team had engaged the enemy.

They heard desperate shouts, screams and gunfire. Men dying, one by one, just as had happened to the SEAL team.

Listening in, Mother stopped briefly at a security checkpoint – a small computer console sunk into an alcove in the wall. These computers were linked to the *George Washington*'s security system. Mother could see the cross-section of the ship and pinpoint where intruders were.

Right now – to the sound of the Airborne team's desperate struggle – she could see the large swarm of red dots at the right-hand end of the image overwhelm the Airborne team.

In the centre of the digital image of the *George Washington* was her own team, heading for the hangar.

But then there was a sudden change in the image.

A number of the 400-strong swarm of dots – a subgroup of perhaps forty dots – broke away from the main group at the bow and started heading *back* toward the main hangar.

'Scarecrow,' Mother called, 'I've got hostiles coming back from the bow. Coming back toward us.'

'How many?' *And how did they know . . .*

'Thirty, maybe forty.'

'We can handle forty of anything. Come on.'

They continued running as the final words from the Airborne team came in. Condor shouting, *'Jesus, there are just too ma— Ahhh!'*

Static.

Then nothing.

The Marine team kept moving.

At the rear of the team, Sanchez came alongside the youngest member of Schofield's unit, a twenty-one-year-old corporal named Sean Miller. Fresh-faced, fit and a science-fiction-movie nut, his nickname was Astro.

'Yo, Astro, you digging this?'

Astro ignored him, just kept peering left and right as he moved.

Sanchez kept on. 'I'm telling you, kid, the captain's lost it.'

Astro turned. 'Hey. Pancho. Until *you're* unbeaten on an R7, I'll follow the cap'n.'

R7 stood for Rojo-7. This was a special forces exercise where teams competed against each other in combat situations. In 2004 the exercises had been held in Florida at the same time as a huge Joint Task Forces exercise.

Sanchez said, 'Hey, hey, hey. The Scarecrow's wasn't the only team to go unbeaten at R7. The Buck was unbeaten as well.'

The Buck was Captain William Broyles, known as the Buccaneer, a great warrior. He was the former leader of what was known to be the best Marine Force Reconnaissance Unit, Unit 1.

Sanchez went on: 'Fact is, the Buck won the overall exercise on points because he beat the other teams faster than the Scarecrow did. Shit, the only reason the Scarecrow got a draw with the Buck was because he evaded the Buck's team till the entire exercise timed out.'

'A draw's a draw.' Astro shrugged. 'And . . . er . . . didn't you used to be in the Buck's unit?'

'Damn straight,' Sanchez said. 'So was Bigfoot. But they disbanded Unit 1 a few months ago and we've been shuffled from team to team ever since, ending up with you guys for this mess.'

'So you're biased.'

'So I'm careful. And you should be, too, 'cause we might just be working under a boss who's not firing on all cylinders.'

'I'll make up my own mind. Now shut up, we're here.'

Sanchez looked forward, and stopped.

They'd arrived at the main hangar deck.

MAIN HANGAR DECK, USS *GEORGE WASHINGTON*

Shane Schofield and his men walked onto a catwalk suspended from the ceiling about a hundred feet above the floor. The catwalk appeared to end at a huge steel wall built from floor to ceiling. In fact the catwalk ran the whole length of the hangar deck, continuing on the other side of the wall right to the end of the enormous space. In the event of the ship taking in water, the steel wall divided the hangar into two bays and would prevent one side from flooding.

An indoor space the size of two football fields lay beneath him, stretching away to the left and right. Normally it would have been filled with assorted planes, Humvees and trucks.

But not today.

Today it was very different.

Schofield recalled Gator's description of the hangar deck: *'It's like an indoor battlefield. I've got artificial trenches, some low terrain, even an observation tower set up inside the hangar.'*

It was true.

The hangar deck had indeed been made into a mock battlefield.

However it had been done, it had taken a huge effort, involving several million tons of earth. The end result: something that looked like the Somme in World War One – a great muddy field, with four parallel trenches, low hills and one high steel-legged observation tower that rose 20 metres off the ground right in the centre of the enormous space.

The regular residents of the hangar – some of the leftover planes of the *George Washington* – lay parked at the stern end of it: two F-14 Tomcats, an Osprey and some trucks.

The observation tower was connected to the catwalk on which Schofield and his men were standing by a steep bridge. This bridge, like the catwalk, was suspended from the ceiling.

Schofield said, 'Astro and Bigfoot, cover the catwalk to the north of this bridge. Sanchez and Cheese, you watch the south side. Call me on the UHF channel on the radio the second you see anything.'

Along with the rest of his team, Schofield then crossed the bridge to the viewing platform at the top of the observation tower.

Broken computers and torn printouts littered the platform. Blood was everywhere.

'What the hell was this place?' Hulk asked.

'An observation post. From here, the big guys watched the exercises down on the hangar floor,' Mother said.

'But the exercises, it seems, went seriously wrong,' Schofield said, examining a printout. Like most of the other material lying around, it was headed:

PROJECT STORMTROOPER
SECURITY CLASS:
TOP SECRET-2X
DARPA/US ARMY

'Stormtrooper . . .' he read aloud.

Movement out of the corner of his eye.

Schofield spun – just as an attacker came bursting out of a locker at the back of the observation platform.

Six guns moved as one, locking onto the attacker. But not a single one fired – since the 'attacker' had fallen to his knees, sobbing.

He was a young man, about thirty, dressed in a lab coat and wearing horn-rimmed glasses. A computer nerd, dirty and terrified.

'Don't shoot! Please don't shoot! Oh, my God, I'm so glad you're here! You have to help me! We lost control! They wouldn't obey us any more! And then they—'

'Hold it, hold it,' Schofield said, stepping forward. 'Calm down. Start again. What's your name?'

'My n-name is . . . Pennebaker. Zak Pennebaker.' He peered around fearfully.

Schofield saw the name matched the one on the man's ID badge. The ID badge also featured clearance levels and a silver disc at its base – an odd addition to a name tag. Schofield had never seen one before. *Radiation meter, perhaps?*

'I'm a DARPA scientist. *Please*, you gotta get me out of here, off this boat, before they come back.'

'Not until you tell us what this project was.'

'I can't.'

'Let me put it another way: you tell us about the project or we leave you here.'

Zak Pennebaker didn't need an invitation to work that out. He blurted out everything.

'It started out as a project to make super-soldiers. We used human subjects and tried drugs, biomechanics, and grafting microchips into their brains to improve their ability and motivation to fight. But it didn't work out very well. The ape subjects, however, worked very, *very* well.'

'*Ape* subjects?' Mother said in disbelief.

'Yes, apes. Gorillas. African mountain gorillas to be precise. They're twice as strong as human beings and the grafting technology worked perfectly with them.'

'Not quite perfectly,' Hulk said, pointing to the observation platform.

'Well, no, no. Not in the end,' Pennebaker mumbled. 'But when the apes took so well to the training, the project changed from a special forces operation to a frontline troop-replacement project.'

'What do you mean?' Schofield asked.

'Gorillas are the ultimate frontline trooper. They're lethal and vicious, yet totally obedient. And best of all, if they die in battle, there'll be no more letters from a grateful nation to grieving parents. No more one-legged veterans protesting in Washington D.C. Hell, no more veterans full stop – it would save the government billions. If you're a general, facing a frontal assault, it's a lot easier to send a thousand purpose-bred apes to their deaths than fresh-faced farm boys from Idaho.

'And that's the best part. We bred the gorillas ourselves in labs, so we aren't even thinning the natural population or committing some crime against nature. They are the first custom-made, artificially produced armed force in the history of mankind. You could send them into hostile territory and they'd never question the order. Hell, you could send them on complete suicide missions and they'd never complain.'

'How the hell did you manage that?' Hulk asked.

'Grafting technology,' Schofield answered.

Pennebaker seemed surprised that Schofield would know about this. 'Yes. That's correct.'

'What's grafting technology?' Mother asked.

Schofield said, 'You attach – or *graft* – a microchip to the brain of your subject. The chip attaches to the brain and becomes part of it. Grafting technology has allowed totally

41

paralysed patients to communicate via computers. Their brain engages with the chip and the chip sends a signal to the computer. But . . . I've heard it can also work the other way round.'

'That's right,' Pennebaker said. 'When an outside agent uses a grafted microchip to control the *subject*.'

'Jesus, Mary and Joseph.' Mother sighed. 'Pennebaker, you must have read a million books in college filled with words I couldn't even understand, but didn't you just once think about reading *Frankenstein*?'

Pennebaker responded, 'You have to believe me. The results were amazing, at least at the start. The apes were perfectly obedient and shockingly effective. We taught them how to use weapons. We even created modified M-4 assault rifles for them to fit their bigger hands. But even when they lost their guns, they were *still* deadly – they could crush a man's head with their bare hands or bite his whole face off.'

As Pennebaker spoke, Schofield looked at his four men guarding the catwalk. None of them had moved.

He tuned the radio to the UHF channel. 'Astro? Cheese? Any contacts?'

'Not a thing from the north, sir.'

'Ditto, the south, sir. It's too quiet here.'

Schofield turned back to Pennebaker. 'You're saying you tested these things against human troops?'

Pennebaker bowed his head. 'Yes. Against three companies of Marines we had brought here from Okinawa. What are you guys?'

'Marines,' Mother growled.

Pennebaker swallowed. 'The apes destroyed them. Down on the battlefield and also on the island proper. We had five hundred gorillas versus six hundred Marines. The gorillas lost heaps in the first exchange, but they just took their losses without a backward step. The chips in their heads don't allow for useless emotions like fear. So the apes just kept coming, climbing over the piles of their dead, until the Marines were toast.'

Mother pushed her face – and pistol – into Pennebaker's. 'You call a Marine *toast* again, fucknut, and I'll waste you right now.'

Schofield said softly, 'And fear is not a useless emotion, Mr Pennebaker.'

Pennebaker shrugged. 'Whatever. You see, it was then the apes started doing unexpected things. Strategic thinking; killing their own wounded. And then there were the more *unseemly* things, like cutting the hands off their enemies and piling them up.'

'Yeah, heard about that,' Mother said. 'Charming.'

'And then they turned on you,' Schofield said.

'And then they turned on us. The most unexpected thing of all. While we were looking the other way, watching the exercise, they sent a subteam to take this tower. Took us by surprise. They're smart, *tactical*. They out-thought us and now they own this ship and the island. Marines, welcome to the end of your lives.'

'We're not dead yet,' Schofield said.

'Oh, yes you are. You're completely screwed,' Pennebaker said. 'You have to understand: *you can't beat these things*. They are stronger than you are. They are faster. Christ, they've been *bred* to fight for longer, to stay awake for ninety-six hours at a time. If they don't kill you straight away, they'll just wait you out and get you later, like they did with the last few regular Marines. Add to that their technological advantages – Signet-5 radio-locaters, surgically implanted digital headsets – and your graves are practically dug. These things are the *evolution* of the modern soldier, Captain, and they're so damned good, even their makers couldn't control them.'

Mother shook her head. 'How do you geniuses manage to keep doing things like this?'

Without warning, a voice exploded in Schofield's earpiece: Astro's voice.

'Oh God, no, we missed them! There! Shit! Captain! Duck!'

Standing with his back to the main hangar, Schofield didn't turn to confirm Astro's warning, he just obeyed, trusting his man. He dived to the floor – a bare instant before a black man-sized *creature* came swooping in over his head and slammed to the floor right where he'd been standing.

Had Schofield stayed upright for even a nanosecond longer, the knife in the creature's hand would have slashed his throat.

The creature now stood before him and for

the briefest of moments Schofield got a look at it.

It was indeed an ape, perhaps five and a half feet tall, with straggly black fur. But this was no ordinary jungle gorilla. It wore a lightweight helmet, which had an orange visor on the front that covered the animal's eyes. On the helmet's rear were some stubby antennae. Body armour covered its chest and shoulders. Wrist guards protected its arms. And in a holster on its back was a modified M-4.

Goddamn.

But that was all Schofield got to see, for just then the ape bared its jaws and launched itself at him – just as it was shot to bits, about a million bits, as Mother and Hulk nailed it with their MP-7s, turning the ape into red spray.

Then Astro yelled: *'Marines! Look sharp! They're not coming in via the catwalk! They're coming at you from across the ceiling!'*

Schofield stood and spun round, looking up at the ceiling. What he saw was about forty black gorillas all dressed in military gear. They were moving across the ceiling using the pipes, lights and pulleys that were attached to it.

Schofield watched, becoming more horrified

as the nearest ape – hanging upside down from three of its four limbs, raised its free hand and levelled an M-4 rifle at the tower and opened fire.

SECOND ASSAULT

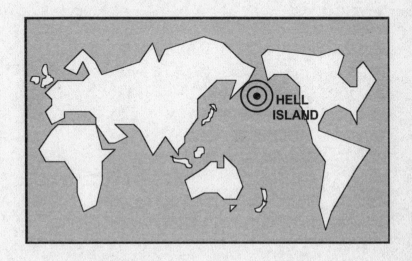

HELL ISLAND

1600 HOURS

1 AUGUST 2005

MAIN HANGAR DECK, USS *GEORGE WASHINGTON*

THE APES MOVED ACROSS the ceiling with incredible speed, at a pace faster than a human could run across land. And the fact that they were more than 30 metres off the floor didn't seem to worry them at all.

Schofield's Marines opened fire and the first three gorillas dropped off the ceiling in explosions of blood, shrieking.

But the others just kept on coming, firing as they came.

The man beside Schofield, a young private, was hit square in the face and was thrown backwards. Another Marine was hit in the chest and flopped to the floor.

Then the force of apes split in the middle and started to fan out around the tower, like an ocean wave washing around a rock.

Mother was busy unleashing a deadly volley of fire at three of the beasts when a fourth ape landed with a thud on the observation platform right next to her and threw itself at her from the side.

Ape and Mother went sprawling across the floor, in a violent and desperate struggle. Since both had lost their guns in the tumble, this would be the worst kind of battle: hand-to-hand combat to the death.

Mother was strong, but the ape was stronger, and it quickly got the upper hand, head-butting her hard and then throwing her against a nearby table. With a roar, the ape hurled itself at her, aiming its bared teeth at her nose . . .

. . . only to catch one of Mother's grenades in its mouth. She had whipped it around and jammed it into the creature's jaws.

'Get a taste of this,' she said, rolling away a second before the confused gorilla's head simply exploded into a shower of red spray.

The gorilla force was gathering above the observation tower, raining automatic fire from all sides on the Marines.

Then the gorillas started leaping down onto the observation platform. In one instance four of them tackled *one* of Schofield's Marines, taking him down with their bare hands. One gorilla was ripped to shreds by the Marine's final spray of fire, but the rest got him. The unlucky Marine fell, screaming, covered by the frenzied apes.

The gorillas' suicidal strategy meant their numbers were starting to drop fast. Forty had quickly become twenty, but even then the numbers game was still in their favour: Schofield's ten-man Marine team was now down to seven, three on the tower, plus the four over on the catwalk, supplying cover fire.

'Marines!' Schofield called. 'Get off this tower! Back to the catwalk! Now!'

He began to retreat – pushing Zak Pennebaker in front of him. As he did he managed to aim his gun and drop three gorillas that had just landed on the observation platform. But the three apes didn't die; they clawed after him despite their wounds and it took *six more shots* to kill them all.

There was a gurgled scream as the Marine beside Schofield was shot in the throat. He fell, and even though he was already mortally wounded, two nearby gorillas came down on him in a fury, firing their guns into his body, tearing at his face with their hands.

Jesus . . . Schofield's eyes went wide.

Of the six Marines who had stepped onto the tower, only he and Mother had survived. They began crossing the bridge to the catwalk, sheltering Pennebaker between them and chased by the twenty gorillas.

Once they got back to the catwalk, Schofield checked their options. The gorillas were still moving over the ceiling, using the pipes to get them across. They were making for the other end of the catwalk.

Schofield turned to his men. 'Let's go,' he said, and the six remaining Marines – Schofield, Mother, Astro, Sanchez, Bigfoot and Hulk – charged along the catwalk in the opposite direction to the gorillas, their boots clanging on the high suspended walkway.

Seconds later, the gorillas arrived at the catwalk and started their pursuit, exchanging fire with the last man in the Marine squad, Sanchez.

Moving in the lead of this desperate bunch of soldiers, Mother came to the steel wall first and threw open the door. She saw that the catwalk continued beyond it in a straight line, only now it was suspended over a second hangar bay. Mother froze in the doorway.

'God have mercy . . .' she breathed.

Schofield came up beside her, looked beyond the doorway into the forward hangar bay.

'Oh my God . . .'

This hangar bay contained no indoor battle-field, but housed regular planes and trucks and jeeps on its wide bare floor.

What it did have, however, were about 350 gorillas standing on the floor of the gigantic space. All around them were the grisly remains of Condor's 82nd Airborne unit.

Schofield looked down in time to see the lead ape pull Condor's rifle from the Airborne leader's dead hands, raise it into the air and roar in triumph.

Then – Schofield didn't know how, it was almost as if it had a sixth sense – the lead ape turned and looked up and stared directly into Shane Schofield's eyes.

It was like stumbling into a lion's den while the lion was eating a meal.

The lead ape let out a load roar and the crowd of gorillas around him moved as one in response: they started scaling every avail-able ladder. Some even climbed the giant dividing wall itself. They were all now heading for the catwalk on which Schofield's team stood.

Running in the rear, Sanchez arrived at the door in the dividing wall just as Schofield came charging *back out* through it.

'What—'

'We're going back this way,' Schofield said, not even stopping.

'But they're still back there—'

'We've got a better chance against this group than that one.' Schofield and the others shoved past Sanchez.

Ever doubtful, Sanchez *had* to look for himself and saw the mass of apes surging up at him from the forward hangar bay. 'Goddamn . . .'

'Sanchez!' Schofield called back. 'When you decide to join us, lock that door behind you!'

Sanchez locked the door and jammed the lock for good measure. Then he turned and followed the others.

Schofield ran back down the high catwalk – having squeezed past his team until he was back in the lead. Once again he began heading toward the original smaller squad of gorillas.

'Mother! Astro! Bigfoot! Rolling leapfrog

formation!' he called as he went by. 'Full auto. Mow 'em down.'

He was running down the catwalk at full tilt now, his MP-7 raised and firing. He took down three of the twenty apes charging toward him.

Once his gun went dry, he hit the deck, dropping to his belly, allowing Mother to jump over him and do the same – run and fire with a fury.

She nailed six more, then dropped to *her* belly . . . at which point Astro hurdled her, gun blazing.

Then Astro ducked and Bigfoot hurdled him. In this way the four of them destroyed the small gorilla force in what was a classic textbook move. Now they were alone in the giant space.

Not for long.

The larger gorilla force had started banging on the door in the dividing wall. Then, with a loud mechanical groaning, a huge door down on the floor began to roll upwards, opening . . .

'Scarecrow! What do we do?' Mother yelled. 'I've never been in this kind of situation before!'

'We stay alive, any way we can! *There!*'

He pointed at the furthest elevator on the starboard side of the hangar. It was a giant thing, a massive open-air platform designed to lift entire planes up from the hangar deck to the flight deck.

A gangway branched off the outer edge of the massive elevator, stretching down to the dock of Hell Island.

'The gangway!' Schofield called. 'Go!'

The six Marines hurried along the catwalk until they came to a long rope ladder which reached to the floor of the hangar. They slid down it one after the other, Schofield leading the way.

The main gorilla force was flooding into the bay through a ground-level door in the huge steel wall like bats out of hell. Their numbers were incredible. They *poured* through the door, then climbed over the muddy fake battlefield, up and over the trenches and the barbed wire, guns firing, jaws bared.

It was, quite simply, the most fearsome assault force Schofield had ever seen.

These gorillas were armed, enraged and completely lacking any fear of death. Any human force that saw this army would be likely to turn to jelly with fear.

Schofield was almost at the elevator, only

50 metres away, when something completely unexpected happened.

The elevator began to rise.

'Oh, no . . . *No!*'

The great platform lifted fast. As the elevator rose up and out of sight, heading for the flight deck, the gangway leading to dry land dropped down into the water with an ungainly splash.

'They can work the elevators,' Bigfoot gasped. 'Son of a bitch!'

'Next plan?' Sanchez said.

'Stay moving,' Schofield said, scanning the area for another way to escape. 'Always stay moving. While you're moving, you're still in the game. If you stop, you're dead. Never stop.'

As he spoke, he saw two large trucks parked over by the wall. He also saw the large ramp evidently leading up to the flight deck. 'Marines! Those trucks! Get in and make for the flight deck!'

The squad split up, racing for the two trucks. They were five-ton troop transports, their backs covered with canvas.

Schofield and Bigfoot dived into the cab of one truck; Mother, Astro, Hulk and Sanchez jumped into the other.

As Schofield slid into the driver's seat, he spun round to check on the scientist, Pennebaker, to see if he was keeping up – only to see Zak Pennebaker skulking into a side door of the hangar 30 metres away, *on his own*. It seemed like he preferred to handle this disaster by himself. Schofield watched as he disappeared through the door.

'What the . . .' Schofield frowned. But he didn't have time to think about that problem. The apes had cleared the battlefield and were now advancing across the open deck like the army of darkness.

Schofield gunned the engine.

The two trucks roared into life and shot off the mark, heading for the ramp that led to the flight deck. It was a deadly journey as the ramp's wide entrance lay back toward the oncoming ape army, about halfway between the two forces. The Marines had to drive toward the apes, racing them to get to the entrance first.

It was a dead heat. Mother's truck reached the ramp just as the ape force did.

The first gorillas launched themselves at her truck, clutching onto any handhold they could find. Eight of them got a grip on it.

It was worse for Schofield.

Driving behind Mother, he got to the ramp entrance two seconds too late. The ape army swarmed across the ramp, blocking it, and suddenly he had a decision to make: plough through the mass of hairy black beasts or turn away.

Screw it.

He ploughed right into the horde of apes, slamming through their ranks with his big five-ton truck.

Squeals, shrieks . . . and gunfire as the apes opened fire.

A barrage of bullets shattered Schofield's windscreen – apes went flying left and right – some banging against the truck's bullbar, others disappearing under it, more still grabbing onto its sides and climbing aboard – the truck bumping and bouncing.

Schofield ducked as gunfire hit his cab, slamming into the headrest of his seat.

It was too much fire. Driving head-on toward it, he couldn't keep control of the truck. He couldn't get onto the ramp. He yanked on the steering wheel, veered away from the ape-filled entrance . . . now with no less than twenty-five apes hanging from his truck!

He swung the truck in a wide arc away from the ramp, across the wide area of clear deck.

Suddenly, with a roar, an ape bounced down onto the bonnet of the truck and – *blam!* – Schofield nailed it with one of his two .45 calibre pistols, throwing the creature off the truck.

Then another ape swung in *through* the driver's side window with its gun raised and – *blam!* – Bigfoot fired across Schofield's body, sending the gorilla flying away with a yelp.

Then two more apes hung down from the roof of the cab – their heads appearing upside down and their M-4s extended – only for Schofield to fire repeatedly up into the *ceiling* of the cab, hitting the two apes in their chests through the metal of the roof! The pair of apes went into violent convulsions before sliding off the speeding truck.

'Boss! We can't keep this up!' Bigfoot called. 'It's only a matter of time till they overwhelm us!'

'I know! I know!' Schofield yelled back, searching for an option.

The big truck, absolutely covered by gorillas, swung in a wide circle, flinging some of them clear with the force of the turn.

Then Schofield saw the *port*-side exterior elevator – on the side of the ship which faced the ocean.

Right now it was occupied by an F-14 Tomcat fighter jet, attached to a low towing vehicle.

Schofield's eyes lit up. 'Hang on.' He gunned the engine and broke out of his circular line of travel, cutting a beeline for the port-side elevator.

'What are you doing?'

'Just get ready to jump!'

They hit the open-air elevator doing sixty, just as two more gorillas jumped down onto the truck's running boards and *wrenched off* the doors on either side of the cab – only to be blown away a second later by Schofield and Bigfoot firing across each other.

'Now!' Schofield yelled.

He and Bigfoot dived out of the speeding truck, landing in twin rolls on either side of it . . .

. . . while the truck continued on and shot off the edge of the elevator, sailing through the air, wheels spinning, still covered in a mass of black gorillas, before it crashed down into the sea with a huge splash.

Schofield and Bigfoot lay on the open-air elevator, gasping for breath.

'You okay?' Schofield asked. 'Still got all your limbs?'

'Uh, yeah, I think so . . .'

Schofield spun, to see the full ape army staring at him from the other side of the hangar, 80 metres away.

They roared as one and charged.

'Oh, Christ!'

At the same time as Schofield was sending his truck to a watery grave, Mother's truck was tearing up the ramp to the flight deck, bearing eight apes on its roof and outer flanks, and being chased by about 100 more on foot.

It was like escaping from the underworld, chased by all of its demons.

Mother pushed the accelerator to the floor, slamming the climbing truck into the outer walls of the rampway and losing a couple of apes that way.

At the back of the truck Sanchez, Astro and

Hulk were doing battle with four apes that had just swung inside.

Sanchez shot one in the chest, while Astro disarmed another and kicked it through the side canvas of the truck, but Hulk wasn't so lucky. The other two apes took him on together, and in the scuffle one managed to shoot him in the stomach.

Hulk roared in pain – just as the two apes did something totally unexpected: they yanked him off the back of the speeding truck, jumping with him, without any thought, it seemed, to the injuries they themselves would suffer.

Astro saw it all in a kind of unreal slow motion.

He saw Hulk's eyes go wide as the big man fell onto the ramp behind the truck, gripped by the two gorillas.

Then he saw the army of apes overwhelm Hulk, using their M-4s as clubs rather than guns. Astro winced as he lost sight of Hulk amid the mass of black fur.

But even then, not every ape stopped to join in the mauling of Hulk – the rest just kept running, climbing over the gorillas battering Hulk's body, still chasing after the fleeing truck.

'Goddamn . . .' Astro breathed.

And then, *wham*! Mother's truck burst into grey daylight, into the pouring rain lashing the flight deck.

The four remaining gorillas on her truck made their move. They gathered on the cab in a coordinated manner – swinging down together from the roof, one at each door, the other two landing on the bonnet of the truck, right in front of Mother, guns up.

'Yikes,' Mother breathed.

There was no escape. No chance.

Except . . .

'Hang on, boys!' she called into her radio.

And with that, she yanked on the steering wheel, bringing the truck into a sharp right-hand turn, a turn that was far too fast for a vehicle of its type.

Gravity played its part.

The truck turned sharply, its inner wheels lifting off the tarmac . . . and it rolled.

The big truck tumbled across the rain-slicked flight deck, sending the apes on its cab and bonnet flying in every direction. Then it landed on its side and slid for a full 20 metres before coming to rest against the lone Super Stallion helicopter on the deck.

Mother crawled out of the truck and raced to its rear.

'You okay?' she called, crouching down.

Sanchez and Astro lay crumpled, bruised and bloody but alive.

'Come on.' Mother peered back at the ramp. 'We gotta keep—'

She cut herself off.

The apes were already at the top of the ramp. A great crowd of them – easily 100 strong – now stood on the deck, in the rain, at the top of the ramp, grunting and snorting and glaring right at her.

Still on her knees, totally exposed, Mother just sighed. 'Game over. We lose.'

The apes charged, raising their guns, pulling the triggers.

Mother shut her eyes.

The sound of gunfire rang out – loud, hard and brutal – and Mother thought this was the last sound she'd ever hear.

Braaaaaaaaaaaaap!

But there was something wrong with this sound. It was too loud for an M-4, too deep. It was the sound of a much larger gun.

67

Crouched at the rear of her overturned truck, Mother hadn't noticed the elevator rise up to deck level behind her.

Nor seen what stood on the elevator: a Tomcat fighter jet, pointing right at her. Sitting in the cockpit of the Tomcat were Shane Schofield and Bigfoot!

Schofield sat in the pilot's seat, gripping the control stick and jamming down on its trigger.

Tracer rounds whizzed by Mother on either side, popping past her ears, before screaming into the crowd of gorillas beyond her, mowing them down.

The first three rows of gorillas fell at once. The others split up, fanned out, looking for cover.

'*Mother!*' Schofield's voice said in her ear. '*Get out of here! I'll hold them off!*'

'Where can we go?' Mother dragged Astro out of the truck and started running, with Sanchez by her side.

'*Get to Casper's door!*' Schofield said cryptically. '*Go over the stern! I'll meet you there!*'

Mother did as she was told, moving to the edge of the flight deck, where she lowered Astro over the side of the ship, down to a safety net hanging just below the deck. She and Sanchez then jumped down after him and disappeared inside a hatch.

That left Schofield and Bigfoot in the Tomcat facing the eighty-strong force of apes.

'Bigfoot! Let's move! Time to get out of here—'

All of a sudden, their fighter started rocking wildly.

Schofield spun in his seat. 'Shit! They must have climbed up the side of the ship!'

The rest of the ape army had climbed up the outside of the ship from the hangar deck and were now clambering over the platform of the elevator.

They swarmed around the plane, clambered up onto it, shook it, hit it, fired at it.

Schofield closed the Tomcat's canopy a split second before it was hit by gunfire. But the canopy was reinforced glass – it could deflect high-velocity air-to-air tracers, so it could handle this small-arms fire, even from up close.

But then one clever gorilla climbed into the towing vehicle that was attached to the Tomcat and started it up.

'Aw, no way, that just ain't fair.' Bigfoot breathed.

Covered in raging apes, and now pulled by the towing vehicle, the Tomcat slowly started moving . . .

. . . toward the edge of the elevator that was open to the sea.

'They're going to tip us over the side!' Bigfoot exclaimed.

Indeed they were.

The Tomcat rolled toward the edge of the elevator, six storeys above the water.

As it did so, the apes on its back started bailing off it, jumping clear. They knew what was about to happen.

'Ah, Captain?' Bigfoot said. 'Any ideas?'

'Yeah. Buckle up.' Schofield was already strapping on his seatbelt.

'Buckle up? How's that going to— Oh!' Bigfoot clutched his belts, and started clasping them together.

The towing vehicle came to the edge of the platform and the ape driving it bailed out just as the vehicle tipped over the edge and hung from the Tomcat's front landing gear.

The ape army did the rest. They pushed the

F-14 until its front wheels lurched off the edge and the entire plane – with Schofield and Bigfoot in it – fell, off the carrier, plunging 30 metres *straight down* to the water far below.

The instant the Tomcat fell off the edge, the canopy of the fighter blew open and the F-14's two ejection seats shot up out of the plane.

The ejection seats – with Schofield and Bigfoot on them – rocketed up into the sky above the aircraft carrier. Meanwhile the Tomcat went down, the plane falling in a clumsy tumbling heap down the side of the ship and into the water, where it landed with a great splash and immediately began to sink.

Schofield and Bigfoot flew high into the air before they disengaged their flight seats and opened the parachutes that were attached to their seatbelts.

As the two of them floated back down to earth, they scanned the huge force of apes on the deck of the carrier. They looked like an army of ants swarming over the aft runway.

Then suddenly gunshots started to zing past Schofield's head, tearing through his chute.

'Where to now?' Bigfoot asked over the UHF.

Schofield pursed his lips, thinking fast. His eyes fell on the chunky Super Stallion helicopter in the centre of the flight deck.

'It's time to even the score a little. Follow me.'

He angled his chute back toward the carrier.

Schofield touched down on the middle of the flight deck. Bigfoot landed soon after, near the controls for the aircraft catapult launchers.

The apes charged forward, roaring, firing, rampaging.

'Stay here,' Schofield ordered before racing across the open deck to the massive Super Stallion.

Hunched in the pouring rain, he did something near the front of the chopper, out of Bigfoot's sight, before he came back round and charged into the helicopter via its right-side door. He slammed the door shut an instant before the gorillas arrived and started banging on the side of the chopper, massing around it.

Inside the Super Stallion, Schofield hustled into the cockpit, shutting its door behind him and locking it.

Watching from the outside, taking cover

72

behind the catapult launcher, Bigfoot was confused.

What was Schofield doing?

But then something even more confusing occurred.

The rear loading ramp of the Super Stallion folded open.

Naturally, the apes stormed it, fifty of them rushing inside, hungry for Schofield's blood.

Bigfoot frowned. *What on earth is he—*

'*Bigfoot!*' Schofield's voice said over the UHF radio channel. '*After you do what I ask, get down to Casper's door and find the others. I'll meet you there.*'

'Casper's d—? Oh yeah, sure,' Bigfoot said. 'But what do you want me to do now?'

'*Simple. Initiate catapult no.1.*'

'What!'

At that moment, Schofield brought the rear loading ramp back up, closing it and *trapping* the fifty-odd apes that had gone inside.

It was then that Bigfoot saw what Schofield had done at the *front* of the chopper: via a tie-down chain, Schofield had attached the helicopter to the carrier's no.1 launch catapult.

'You have got to be kidding!' Bigfoot said.

'Uh, now please, Bigfoot. They're about to break down the cockpit door.'

'Right.'

Bigfoot hit a switch on the launch console, igniting catapult no.1.

The Super Stallion hurtled down the length of the runway at a speed no helicopter had gone before. The steam-driven catapult shot it down the tarmac at an astonishing 160 kilometres an hour!

The great chopper's landing wheels snapped off after about 30 metres and the helicopter *slid* the rest of the way, *on its belly*, sparks flying everywhere, the ear-piercing shriek of metal scraping against the flight deck filling the air.

And then . . . *shoom!* . . . the Super Stallion shot off the bow of the *George Washington*, soaring out from the flight deck for a full 50 metres, hanging in the air for a moment before it arched downward, falling toward the sea.

A second before it hit the ocean, a human figure could be seen leaping from one of its cockpit windows, jumping clear of the falling helicopter, hitting the water at the same time it did, but safely alongside it.

The helicopter came down with a massive

splash and as the splash subsided, it could be seen bobbing slowly in the water.

And then it began to sink.

Terrified shrieks could be heard from within it – the cries of the trapped gorillas.

Ten seconds later, the Super Stallion went under, with its cargo of murderous apes, never to rise again.

Shane Schofield trod water for a few moments, staring at what he'd just done. Then he started swimming back towards the ship, heading for the bow.

Once there, he pulled a bottle from his combat belt – a compact bottle-sized air tank fitted with a mouthpiece. He jammed it into his mouth and went underwater.

Within a minute, he arrived at a little-known entrance to the carrier, one located 15 metres below the waterline: a submarine docking door.

All Marines referred to this airlock door on aircraft carriers as the spooks' door. It had been designed to allow small submarines to dock at it, and return what were called 'long-range reconnaissance troops' to the ship – spies in other words.

Schofield knocked loudly on the door in Morse code, punching out, 'Mother. You there?'

At first there was no reply and Schofield's heart began to beat a little faster, before suddenly there came a muffled knocking from the other side.

'As always.'

THIRD ASSAULT

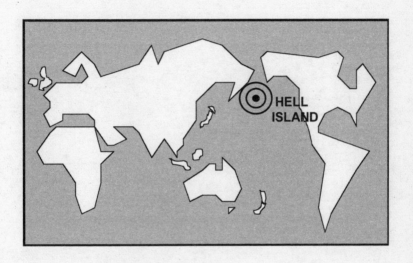

HELL ISLAND

1745 HOURS

1 AUGUST 2005

MAIN HANGAR DECK, USS *GEORGE WASHINGTON*

SCHOFIELD'S TEAM SAT IN a grim silent circle beside the airlock that was Casper's door, deep within the bowels of the carrier.

There were only five of them now.

Schofield, Mother, Sanchez, Bigfoot and Astro.

Schofield sat on his own a short distance from the other four, head bowed, deep in thought . . . and dripping wet. He'd taken his anti-flash glasses off and was rubbing his eyes.

'What the hell are we gonna do?' Sanchez moaned. 'We're on an island in the middle of the biggest ocean in the world, with three hundred of those *things* hunting us down. We're completely, utterly, abso-fuckin-lutely screwed.'

Astro shook his head. 'There's just too many of them. It's only a matter of time.'

Mother looked over at Schofield – still sitting with his head bent, thinking.

The others followed her gaze, as if waiting for him to say something.

Sanchez misunderstood Schofield's silence for fear. 'Aw, great! He's *frozen up*! Man, I wish I coulda stayed in the Buck's unit.'

'*Hey!*' Mother barked. 'I've just about had a gutful of your complaints, Sanchez. You doubt the Scarecrow one more time and I'll perform my own court martial on you right here. That man's got the coolest head in the game. Cooler than the fucking Buck and way cooler than you, that's for sure. I've seen him think his way out of worse situations than this.'

'Sanchez,' Bigfoot said softly. 'She's right. You shoulda seen him up on the flight deck. He must have taken out forty of those apes from the Tomcat, and then another fifty in the chopper that he tossed off the bow. He's taken care of ninety of them all by himself. Now I know you liked serving with the Buck, but you gotta move on. This guy's not better or worse than the Buck, he's just different. Why don't you cut him a break?'

This was a big moment. Bigfoot was Sanchez's closest friend in the unit and his former teammate under Buccaneer Broyles.

Sanchez scowled. 'I got a question then. In R7 exercises, in Florida, back in 2004, the Buck beat everybody except him.' He jerked a nod at Schofield. 'Led by him, you guys evaded us for forty-one hours, till the exercise was over. How did you manage that for so long?'

'It was all him, all his doing,' said Mother. 'He saw a pattern in the Buck's moves, and once he found that pattern, he could work out every move you guys made. You had the advantage of bigger numbers, but since he could predict your every next move, it didn't matter.'

'What pattern did he see in our moves?'

'Scarecrow realized that the Buck employed the same tactic again and again: he'd always use one subteam to push his opponent toward a larger, waiting, force. You see, that's Scarecrow's biggest talent. He spots patterns, the enemy's patterns, their tactics and strategies and then he uses those patterns against them.'

'But he didn't use anything against us in R7,' Sanchez said. 'He just avoided us. He didn't *hurt* us in any way.'

'Oh, yes, he did,' Mother said. 'By evading

81

you guys till the end of the exercise, he deprived you of the one thing you wanted most of all: a clear win.'

Sanchez growled. This was true.

Her point made, Mother turned to look back at Schofield – only to find him gazing directly back at her, his eyes alive.

She said, 'Well, hey there, handsome. What's up? Whatcha thinking?'

It was as if a light bulb had gone off above his head.

'The Buck . . .' he said.

'What about him?'

'He's here. Now. Commanding these ape troops.'

Schofield spoke quickly.

'Think back. In the viewing tower above the indoor battlefield, the apes on the ceiling drove us *forward*, toward the other force of apes in the forward hangar. The *larger* force.

'Then in the aft hangar, they let us try for the port-side elevator but then removed it, knowing we'd have to come *back* through their larger force. They were always driving us toward the larger numbers. It would also explain why the Corps disbanded the Buck's unit a few months ago – he was being assigned to a special mission. This one.'

Astro said, 'But that scientist, Pennebaker, said the exercise had gone pear-shaped. If the Buck was here, he'd be dead, too, killed by the gorillas.'

'And where's Pennebaker now?' Schofield asked. 'He was last seen ditching us when we were all trying to get away. Either he felt he was safer on his own – unlikely – or he was part of something bigger, a messenger sent to give us information and maybe increase our fear. Mother, gentlemen, I'm not convinced the "exercise" here at Hell Island went pear-shaped at all. In fact, I'm starting to wonder if it's still going . . . and we're a part of it.'

There was a silence.

Sanchez said, 'Okay. So if the Buck's here, where is he?'

'Somewhere on the boat?' Astro suggested.

'No, I don't think so.' Schofield swapped a look with Mother. 'Remember the power being drained off the ship?'

Mother nodded. 'I agree.'

'What are you two talking about?' Sanchez asked.

83

Schofield said, 'Back on the bridge, we detected power going off the ship and onto the island. The Buck – and whoever else is controlling this ape army – is somewhere on Hell Island.'

He stood, putting his silver anti-flash glasses back on, now looking more lethal than ever.

'Knowledge is a wonderful thing. Now that we've figured some of this out, it's time to turn the tables.'

Schofield waited till dusk to leave the *George Washington*.

If he was going to take on the island, the cover of darkness would be necessary. It also gave him a chance to do some research.

He sent Mother and Astro to find any maps of Hell Island. They found some in one of the staterooms. In the background they could constantly hear the howls of the gorillas searching the ship for them.

When they got back, Schofield and his team studied the maps. The most helpful one showed a network of underground tunnels running throughout the island.

'This used to be called Grant Island,' Schofield said, 'until we stormed it in 1943. The

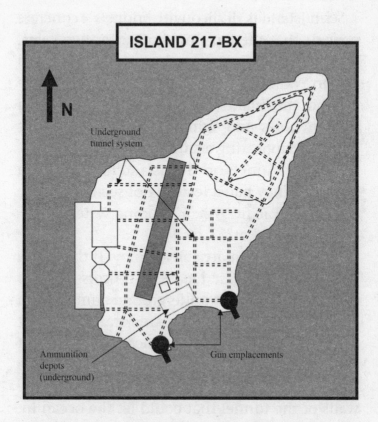

ISLAND 217-BX

N

Underground
tunnel system

Ammunition
depots
(underground)

Gun emplacements

fighting here was some of the bloodiest of the war. Two thousand Japanese defenders fought to the very end on Grant, not giving a single inch – not wanting to give up its airfield. We lost eight hundred Marines taking it. Thing was, we almost lost a lot more.'

'What do you mean?' Mother asked.

85

'Hell Island is riddled with tunnels – concrete tunnels that the Japanese built over two years, connecting all its gun positions, pillboxes, and ammo dumps. The Japanese could move around the island unseen, popping up from hidden holes and firing at point-blank range before disappearing again.

'But the tunnels on Hell Island had one extra purpose. They had a feature not seen anywhere else in the Pacific War: a flooding system.'

'What was that?'

'It was the ultimate suicide ploy. If the island was taken, the last Japanese officers were to retreat to the lowest underground ammunition chamber – followed by the American forces. But from that chamber the Japanese could seal off the entire tunnel system and then open two huge ocean gates – floodgates built into the walls of the tunnel that could let the ocean in. The tunnel system would flood, killing both the Japanese and all the Americans trapped inside. Kind of like a final "screw you" to the victorious American force.'

'Did the Japs use those gates in 1943?' Sanchez asked.

'They did. But a small team of special-mission

Marines braved the rising waters. Using breathing equipment they were able to close the ocean gates, saving five hundred Marines.'

'How do you know this?' Bigfoot asked.

Schofield smiled weakly. 'My grandfather was a member of that special team. His name was Lieutenant Michael Schofield. He led the team that held back the ocean.'

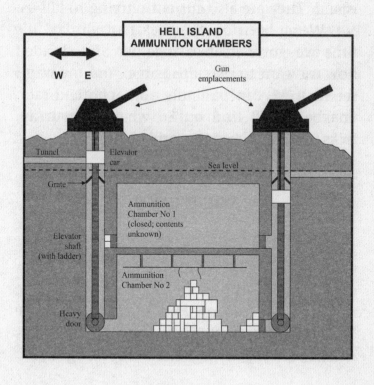

87

Schofield leaned back, staring at the map.

'The ammunition chambers . . .' he said. 'If they're like other World War Two chambers, they're big, hall-sized caverns. If we could lure the apes into one of them, we could seal them *all* inside and – hmmm . . .'

'What about finding the Buck and his control centre?' Sanchez said.

'Too risky. They could be anywhere on the island. They are also currently trying to kill us. No. We've been on the back foot all day. It's time we got ourselves together and decided how we want to play this game. And the way I see it, if we can pull this off,' Schofield said, 'maybe they'll find us. So what do you say, folks? Want to become gorilla bait?'

THE ISLAND

At exactly six p.m., the five Marines left the *George Washington* via the spooks' door, swam over to the nearby shore and, for the first time that day, set foot on Hell Island. The *George Washington* loomed above them in the darkness, a dark shadow against the evening sky.

Schofield and his team quickly found an entrance to the tunnel system – a sixty-year-old cracked archway that stank of decay, dust and the fearful sweat of soldiers long gone.

Beyond the old concrete arch all they could see was inky darkness.

Before they entered the tunnels, Schofield stopped them.

'Okay, hold here for a moment. There's only one way this can work, and that's if they're right behind us.'

He reached for his throat-mike and pressed his radio's 'ON' button, opening up his regular radio channel.

'But they'll know where we are.' Astro said, alarmed.

'That's the whole point, kiddo,' Mother said.

Schofield keyed his radio, put on a worried voice: 'Delta Leader, come in! Flash . . . Flash Gordon! You still alive out there? This is Scarecrow. Please respond!'

He got no reply from the Delta team.

But he did get another kind of response.

A terrifying howl echoed out from the flight deck of the *George Washington*.

His call had been detected.

The gorillas were coming.

And they didn't take long getting there.

They swarmed off the *George Washington*, an army of fast-moving shadows.

Zeroing in on Schofield's radio signal, the 300 apes swarmed to the tunnel entrance, howling, growling and roaring.

Schofield's team charged into the tunnels, pursued by the monsters. It was scary enough moving through the damp, concrete passages – but doing it with an army of deadly creatures on your tail was even worse.

'This way,' Schofield said, referring to his map of the tunnel system.

He was heading for the two massive gun emplacements on Hell Island. The two big guns were set on a pair of cliffs pointing east and south, designed to drive off any approaching fleet.

Actually, that wasn't entirely correct: he was heading for the ammunition chambers buried *underneath and in between* the gun emplacements.

Through the tunnels they ran.

The gorillas caught up, firing and roaring – and Schofield's team fired back as they ran, picking off the apes, never slowing down. To slow down was to die.

Then suddenly they came to a T-junction, where there was a large elevator.

'We're beneath the first gun emplacement,' Schofield said. 'This elevator was used to feed ammunition to the guns from the chambers down below.'

Like the concrete world around it, the elevator was old, rusted beyond repair. It didn't work, but that didn't matter.

'Quickly, down,' Schofield ordered.

One after the other, they swept down a rusty ladder that ran down the elevator shaft.

Moving last of all, Mother grabbed the ladder just as an ape came leaping out of the darkness, grabbing her gun hand.

She turned on the ladder and hurled the gorilla off – allowing it to take her gun, but throwing it out into the elevator shaft. The gorilla sailed down the shaft, into the blackness, its shriek ending with a dull thud.

'Hurry up, people!' Mother called.

They hustled down the ladder.

On the way, Schofield found a huge iron door set into an alcove. Its Japanese markings had been painted over with English: 'AMMUNITION CHAMBER NO 1'.

But there was no access to the door itself. It was obstructed by a cluster of heavy crates and boxes. They'd never get to it.

Down another level and they came to the bottom of the elevator shaft. Schofield found a second huge door marked 'AMMUNITION CHAMBER NO 2'. It was unlocked. There was a large circular pressure door that looked like the entry to a giant safe. It was easily 3 metres in diameter.

Schofield ignored this large door and pushed open the heavy iron door to the ammunition chamber and pulled a glowstick from his belt.

Beside him, Sanchez took out a flare gun and raised it.

'No,' Schofield said sharply. 'Not here.'

He cracked the glowstick – lighting up the room around them with its haunting amber glow – and suddenly Sanchez saw the wisdom of his words.

The room was huge with a high ceiling and concrete walls. The floor space was roughly the size of a basketball court. A network of over-head rails ran along its ceiling, from which dangled chains and hooks. A matching door lay on the far side, leading to a second elevator shaft that fed the other gun emplacement.

And piled up in the centre of the room was a pyramid-shaped stack of wooden crates, 20 metres tall. Each crate was marked in either Japanese or English with 'DANGER: EXPLOSIVES' or 'DANGER: NO NAKED FLAMES'.

In fact, Schofield couldn't recall seeing the word 'danger' so many times in the one place.

'This is what we wanted,' he said in a low voice. 'Come on.'

His team hustled inside.

The apes arrived at the second ammunition chamber a minute later.

The first few must have been advance troops – and for the first time that day they were careful, checking things out, as if suspecting a trap.

They saw Schofield and Mother climbing up the mountain of crates, heading for a catwalk near the ceiling – probably going to join the others up there, although they couldn't be seen. The advance gorillas ducked back outside, to report back to the others.

Thirty seconds later, the attack came.

The sheer strength of it was spectacular.

The ape army *thundered* into the ammo chamber in full assault mode.

Screaming and shrieking, moving fast and spreading out, they stormed the chamber – not firing. The scouts had informed the others of the explosive contents of the room. They'd have to do this *without* guns.

The ape army leapt onto the mountain of crates, coming after Schofield and Mother with the single aim of finishing them off.

Schofield and Mother stayed at the top of the crate mountain, each holding two MP-7 sub-machine guns. They fired them with accuracy, aiming carefully to avoid hitting the ordnance all around them, taking down apes left, right and centre.

Gunfire clattering.

Apes screaming and falling.

Muzzles flashing.

Two against an army.

And the apes just kept coming, live ones clambering over the dead ones, scaling the mountain. For every rank of gorillas that Schofield and Mother mowed down, another *two ranks* stepped forward.

Soon the mountain of crates was crawling with hairy black shapes, all scrambling in a fury to get at the two stubborn Marines at the summit.

'Scarecrow!' Mother called.

'Not yet! We have to wait till they're all inside!'

Then the last apes entered the great underground room, and Schofield called, 'Now!'

As he yelled, the first gorillas reached the summit and clutched at his boots – but they were completely surprised when Schofield and Mother suddenly left their guns and leapt *upwards*, grabbing a pair of chains hanging from the ceiling and using them to swing across the length of the chamber, high above the army of apes swarming over the crates.

Schofield and Mother hit the western wall of the hall and unclipped the clasps on their chains. This caused the chains to unreel from the ceiling, lowering the two of them to the floor of the room right in front of the doorway leading back to the elevator shaft.

'Marines! Now!'

It was then that the other three members of Schofield's unit showed themselves from *behind* some crates near the entrance to the ammo chamber. They stepped partially behind the heavy entry door, and raised their guns to fire back through the gap.

And suddenly the trap became clear.

The *entire* gorilla army was now inside one enclosed space, swarming all over the most explosive mountain in history.

And with Schofield and Mother now down and safe, Bigfoot, Astro and Sanchez aimed their guns at the base of the mountain of crates.

'Fire!' Schofield commanded.

They squeezed their triggers.

But then, from out of nowhere, a voice called, *'Captain Schofield! Don't!'*

Schofield snapped, 'Marines! Hold that order! Do not fire!'

The man's voice was desperate and pleading. It rang out from loudspeakers around the great concrete room and the elevator shaft.

By this time, the apes had started to leave

the mountain of crates, coming back down after Schofield and Mother, but the voice then addressed them, *'Troops! Desist and stand down!'*

Immediately, the apes stopped where they stood, sitting down on their haunches in total absolute obedience.

What moments before had been a frenzied blood-hungry army of apes was now a perfectly behaved crowd of 200 silent mountain gorillas.

And then suddenly *people* appeared behind Schofield's team, moving slowly and calmly, stepping down from the ladder in the elevator shaft: seven men in white lab coats, one officer in uniform and, covering them, a team of Delta commandos: the same ten-man team led by Hugh 'Flash' Gordon that had parachuted in with Schofield's unit earlier that day.

Among the scientists in the white lab coats, Schofield saw Zak Pennebaker, the desperate scientist he'd met earlier.

He also recognized the officer in uniform, which was the khaki day uniform of the United States Marine Corps. He was Captain William 'Buccaneer' Broyles, also known as the Buck.

The leader of the lab-coated crowd stepped

forward. He was an older man, with a mane of flowing white hair, an aged crinkled face and dazzling blue eyes. He spoke with authority.

'Captain Schofield,' he said in a deep voice, 'thank you for your quick response to my plea. My name is Dr Malcolm Knox, scientific consultant to the president, head of the Special Warfare Division at DARPA and overall commander of Project Stormtrooper.'

Knox walked out among the apes – they continued to sit obediently, although they did rock from side to side, fidgeting impatiently, but they did not attack him. Schofield noticed a silver disc on Knox's ID badge – it was exactly the same as the one Pennebaker had been wearing earlier and, Schofield saw, was still wearing now.

Standing with the apes at his back, Knox turned to Schofield and his dirty, blood-covered team.

'Congratulations. You have won this mission, Captain Schofield,' he said.

Schofield said nothing.

'I said, you *won*,' Knox said. 'I commend you on an incredible effort. Indeed, yours was the only team to survive.'

Still Schofield remained silent.

'You really . . . er . . . should all be proud,' said Knox.

'This was a goddamned test,' Schofield said in a low voice, his tone deadly.

'Yes . . . yes it was,' Knox said, slightly unnerved. 'The final test of a new technology—'

Schofield said, 'You pitted your new army against three companies of Marines, and you beat them. But then the higher-ups said you had to beat special forces, didn't they?'

Knox nodded. 'This is correct.'

'So you had us sent here, with the SEALs and the Airborne. You used us as *live bait*. You used us as *human guinea pigs* for a *test*—'

'This gorilla force could save thousands of American lives in future conflicts,' Knox said. 'You, Captain Schofield, are sworn to defend the American people and your fellow soldiers. You were doing exactly that, only in an indirect way.'

'In an indirect way,' Schofield growled. 'I've lost five good men here today, Dr Knox. Not to mention the other Marines, SEALs and Airbornes who also died here in your little experiment. These men had families. They were

99

prepared to die for their country, fighting its *enemies* not its latest fucking weapon.'

'Sometimes a few must be lost for the greater good, Captain,' Knox said. 'This is bigger than you. This is the future of warfare for our country.'

'But your apes *lost* in the end. We had them in the crosshairs and were about to fire the kill-shot.'

'Yes, you did. You most certainly did,' Knox said. 'We needed you in this exercise for precisely that reason: your ability to adapt and change. The apes needed that type of enemy.

'As it stands, however, the gorillas beat everybody. It must be said that you and your victory were based in large part on a few longshots. We know, for example, that 99 per cent of our enemies simply will not have submarine docking doors in carriers and an unusually high level of knowledge of World War Two Japanese tunnel systems. No, based on the results of this test, Project Stormtrooper will most certainly go live, and it will save many men over the years to come.'

Knox started walking around the hall, checking the apes. 'Now, if you don't mind, we have a lot of follow-up to do, and a whole lot of paperwork. A plane has been called from Okinawa to come and take you home. It should be here in a few hours.'

'Paperwork,' Schofield said. 'Men have died and you have paperwork. You guys are something else. Hey, hold it. I have another question.'

Knox stopped.

Schofield nodded at Flash Gordon and the Delta team arrayed around him. 'Why were *they* brought here at all, if they just stayed with you?'

Knox grinned. 'They were brought in to protect my DARPA team. Just in case you *did* happen to survive and got angry with us.'

Knox resumed his casual appraisal of his apes.

Schofield said, 'I should have killed your army when I had the chance.'

'No, you shouldn't have, Captain. What you *should* do is walk away and be proud of yourself. You have done future generations of American farm boys a great service. They will not need to die on the front lines *ever* again. Also, be proud that my apes defeated every other force they faced, but *you* beat *them*. Go home.'

'This is not right. It shouldn't be done this way,' Schofield said.

'What you think, Captain, is not important and does not matter. You are not paid to think about such things. Better brains than yours have discussed these issues. You are paid to fight and to die, and you have successfully done half of that today. Farewell, Captain.' Knox waved Schofield away. 'Specialist Gordon and Captain Broyles will escort you and your men out.'

As he said this, Knox threw Flash Gordon and the Buck a look – unseen by Schofield – that said: *They are not to leave this place alive.*

Gordon nodded. So did the Buck.

The Delta team swooped in on Schofield's five men, surrounding them perhaps a little more tightly than they needed to. Gordon indicated the door. 'Captain . . . if you will.'

Schofield entered the elevator shaft, followed by his team.

Throughout all this, the apes had sat silently, swaying slightly from side to side, as if their lust for blood was being stopped only by the chips in their heads.

Schofield stepped out into the elevator shaft and stood at its base looking at the huge circular safe-like door set into the wall. He headed for the ladder – when suddenly his Delta escorts released the safeties on their guns and aimed them at him and his Marines.

'Hold it right there, Scarecrow,' Gordon said.

'Oh, you *cocksuckers* . . .' Mother said.

'Buck?' Bigfoot asked in surprise.

'Buck, how can you do this?' Sanchez said, turning to his former commander.

Buck Broyles just shrugged. 'Sorry, boys. But you aren't my problem any more.'

'You son of a bitch . . .' Sanchez breathed.

During this exchange, Schofield assessed his options and quickly found there was nothing available. This time, they were well and truly screwed.

But then, as he gazed at his ring of captors, he noticed that every single one of them wore a silver disc clipped to his lapel.

The silver discs, Schofield thought. *That was it . . .*

And suddenly things began to make sense.

That was how you stayed safe from the apes. If you wore a silver disc, the apes couldn't attack you.

The discs were somehow connected to the micro-chips in the apes' heads, probably by some kind of digital radio signal.

A digital radio signal. Schofield sighed inwardly. Like the binary beep signal Mother had picked up earlier. That was how the Buck had been remotely commanding the apes: with digital signals sent directly to the chips in their brains.

The silver discs must work the same way. That must have been how Pennebaker had been able to enter the battle to give Schofield information, without having to fear the apes.

'Mother,' Schofield whispered as he raised his hands above his head, 'still got your radio jammer there?'

'Yeah.'

'Jam radios, all channels, *now.*'

Mother was also in the process of raising her hands – when suddenly she snapped her right hand down and hit a switch on the jammer on her belt, the switch marked: 'SIGNAL JAM: ALL CH'.

The Delta man beside her swung his gun around, but he never fired.

Because right then, another *very loud* sound caught his attention.

The sound of the apes awakening.

The effect of what Mother had done was invisible, but if someone could have *seen* the radio spectrum it would have looked like this: a rippling wave of energy had fanned out from Mother's jamming pack, moving outward from her in a circular motion, like expanding ripples in a pond, hitting every radio device in the area, and turning each device's signal into garbled static.

The result: the silver discs on the ID badges of Knox, the scientists, the Buck and the Delta team all *instantly became useless*.

From his position in the elevator shaft, Schofield saw what happened next in a kind of hyper-real slow motion.

He saw Knox in the ammo chamber with the army of deadly apes looming above him; saw the three apes nearest to Knox suddenly leap down on him, jaws bared, slamming into him, throwing him to the ground, where they fired into him with their M-4s at point-blank range.

In the face of their gunfire, Dr Malcolm Knox was turned into a bloody mess, his body exploding in a million bullet holes. The apes kept firing into him long after he was dead.

Complete madness followed as the rest of the ape army leapt down from their mountain of crates looking for blood.

Different people reacted in different ways.

The scientists in the chamber spun, eyes wide in horror.

In the elevator shaft, the Delta team also turned, shocked, Gordon and the Buck among them.

Schofield, however, was already moving, calling, 'Marines, two hands! Now!'

As for the apes, well, they went apeshit.

Freed from the grip of the silver discs, they launched themselves at the scientists in the ammo chamber, tackling them to the floor, clubbing them with the butts of their guns, tearing them apart – as if all their lives they had been waiting to attack their makers.

Screams and cries rang out.

Zak Pennebaker ran for the door to the elevator shaft, crying, 'Buck! Do something!'

Then he himself was tackled from behind and set upon by six, then eight, then twelve apes.

He disappeared under their bodies, arms waving, screaming in terror, before he was completely overcome by the hairy black monsters.

In the elevator shaft, Flash Gordon and his team of Delta scumbags were caught totally by surprise.

Gordon whirled back to face Schofield, bringing his pistol back round – only to see both of Schofield's pistols aimed directly at his own nose.

'Surprise,' Schofield said.

Blam!

Schofield fired.

The apes were now rushing for the door, all 300 of them, angry and deadly, heading toward Schofield's elevator shaft.

While they did so, Schofield's Marines did battle with the Delta force around them.

It was a short battle.

For Schofield's men had obeyed Schofield's shouted order – 'Marines, two hands!' – so that by now they all held guns in *both* their hands: an MP-7 in one and a pistol in the other.

Suddenly they'd evened the odds against the ten-man Delta squad surrounding them.

The Marines fired as one, spraying bullets outward, dropping the distracted Delta squad around them.

Six of the Delta men were killed instantly by head shots. The other four went down, wounded but not killed.

The only bad guy left standing was the Buck, mouth open, gun held limply at his side, frozen in shock at the unfolding madness around him: the apes were completely out of control; Knox and his scientists were dead; and Schofield's men had just nailed their Delta captors.

A call from Schofield roused him.

'Marines! Up the ladder! Now!'

As his Marines climbed skyward, Schofield grabbed the ladder last of all, shoving past the immobile Buck.

After he was ten feet up, Schofield aimed his pistol at a lever on the big round safe-like door set into the wall of the elevator shaft.

'History lesson for you, Buck,' Schofield said. 'Happy swimming.'

Blam!

Schofield fired, hitting the lever with a spray of sparks.

At which point all hell really broke loose.

The lever snapped downward, into the 'RELEASE' position, and the big ten-foot-wide circular door was instantly *flung* open, swinging inward with massive force, force that came from the weight of ocean water that had been pressing against it from the other side.

This door was one of the floodgates that the Japanese had used in 1943 to flood the tunnels of Hell Island. A door that backed onto the Pacific Ocean itself.

A shocking blast of seawater came rushing in through the circular doorway. It slammed into the Buck, lifting him off his feet and hurling him like a rag doll against the opposite wall of the elevator shaft. The force was so strong that his skull *cracked* when it hit the concrete.

The roar of the ocean flooding into the elevator shaft was deafening. It looked like the spray from a giant fireman's hose, a *ten-foot-wide* spray of super-powerful rushing water.

And one more thing.

The layout of the underground ammo chamber meant that the incoming water flooded *directly into chamber no 2*, where nearly 300 apes now stood, trapped.

The apes scrambled across the chamber, wading waist-deep against the powerful waves of white water pouring into it.

The water level rose fast – the apes howled, struggling against it – but it only took a few seconds for it to hit the upper frame of the doorway to the chamber. It sealed off the chamber completely, cutting off the sounds of the apes screaming in utter terror.

While they could swim short distances, the apes could not swim *underwater*.

They couldn't get out.

Ammunition chamber no 2 of Hell Island would be their tomb – 296 apes, innocent creatures turned into killing machines, would drown in it.

Four apes, however, *did* make it out of the hall before the water completely covered the doorway.

They got to the elevator shaft and started climbing the ladder, heading up and away from the swirling body of ocean water pouring into the concrete shaft beneath them.

Higher up the same ladder, Schofield and his team scaled the shaft as quickly as they could.

The roar of rushing water drowned out all sound for almost thirty seconds until – spookily – the whole shaft suddenly fell silent.

It wasn't that the water had stopped rushing in: it was just that the water *level* had risen above the floodgate. The ocean was still invading the shaft, but from below its own waterline.

'Keep climbing!' Schofield called up to the others, moving last of all. 'We have to get above sea level!'

He looked behind him and saw the four apes chasing them.

Fact: gorillas are much better climbers than human beings.

Schofield yelled, 'Guys! We've got company!'

Three-quarters of the way up the shaft was a large metal grate that folded down across the width of the shaft; notches in its edges allowed it to close around the elevator cables. When closed, it would completely span the shaft, sealing it off. It was one of the gates the Japanese had created to trap intruders down below.

Schofield saw it. 'Mother! When you get to that grate, close it behind you!'

The Marines came to the grate, climbed up past it one at a time – Astro, then Bigfoot, then Sanchez, then Mother.

With a loud clang, Sanchez quickly closed one half of the grate. Mother grabbed the other half, just as Schofield reached it . . .

. . . at the same time as a big hairy hand grabbed his ankle and yanked hard!

Schofield slipped down, dropping six feet below the grate, an ape hanging from his left foot.

'Scarecrow!' Mother shouted.

'Close the grate!' Schofield called.

Behind him, the ocean water was now *charging* up the vertical elevator shaft. It had completely filled the ammo chamber – so it was racing up the only space left for it to go: the much smaller elevator shaft.

'No!' Mother yelled. To shut the grate was to drown Schofield himself.

'You have to!' Schofield shouted back. 'You have to shut them in!'

Schofield glanced down at the crazy gorilla clutching his left foot. The other three apes were clambering up the ladder close behind it.

He levelled his pistol at the gorilla holding him –

Click.

Dry.

'Shit.'

Then suddenly he saw movement out of the corner of his eye. He turned to find someone hovering next to his face, level with his head, someone dangling upended!

Mother.

She was hanging fully stretched, upside-down, her legs held by Sanchez and Bigfoot up at the grate. She held pistols in both hands.

'No heroic sacrifices today, buddy,' she said gruffly to Schofield.

She then opened fire with both her guns, blasting the ape that was holding Schofield to pieces. The ape released him, Mother chucked her guns, grabbed Schofield by his belt and suddenly *whoosh* both Mother *and* Schofield were lifted up the shaft by Sanchez and Bigfoot. Once they were up, Astro slammed down the other half of the grate and snapped shut its lock.

The last three apes and the rising water hit the grate moments later, the water pinning the screaming apes to the grate until it rose past them. It swallowed them, climbing a further ten feet up the shaft, before it suddenly stopped, having come level with the sea outside, and forbidden by the laws of physics from rising any further.

Schofield's Marines gazed down at the sloshing body of water from their ladder above. They were breathless and exhausted but safe, and now the only creatures – man or ape – still breathing on Hell Island.

Four hours later, a lone plane arrived on the landing strip of Hell Island. It was a gigantic Air Force C-17A Globemaster, one of the biggest cargo-lifters in the world. The plane was capable of holding over 200 armed personnel, or perhaps 300 sedated apes.

Its six-man crew were a little surprised to find only five United States Marines – dirty, bloody and battle-weary – waiting on the tarmac to greet it.

Its co-pilot came out and met Schofield and shouted above the whine of the plane's huge jet engines, 'Who the hell are you? We're here to pick up a bunch of DARPA guys, a Delta team, and some cargo that we're not allowed to look at. Nobody said anything about Marines.'

Schofield just shook his head.

'There's no cargo,' he said. 'Not any more. Now, if you don't mind, would you please take us home?'

WORLD BOOK DAY
Quick Reads

Quick Reads are published alongside and in Partnership with BBC RaW.
We would like to thank all our partners on the project for all their help and support:

Department for Education and Skills
Trades Union Congress
The Vital Link
The Reading Agency
National Literacy Trust

Quick Reads would like to thank the Arts Council England and National Book Tokens for their sponsorship.

We would also like to thank the following companies for providing their services free of charge: SX Composing for typesetting all the titles; Icon Reproduction for text reproduction; Norske Skog, Stora Enso, PMS and Iggusend for paper/board supplies; Mackays of Chatham, Cox and Wyman, Bookmarque, White Quill Press, Concise, Norhaven and GGP for the printing.

www.worldbookday.com

Quick Reads

BOOKS IN THE *Quick* Reads SERIES

The Book Boy	Joanna Trollope
Blackwater	Conn Iggulden
Chickenfeed	Minette Walters
Don't Make Me Laugh	Patrick Augustus
Hell Island	Matthew Reilly
How to Change Your Life in 7 Steps	John Bird
Screw It, Let's Do It	Richard Branson
Someone Like Me	Tom Holt
Star Sullivan	Maeve Binchy
The Team	Mick Dennis
The Thief	Ruth Rendell
Woman Walks into a Bar	Rowan Coleman

AND IN MAY 2006

Cleanskin	Val McDermid
Danny Wallace and the Centre of the Universe	Danny Wallace
Desert Claw	Damien Lewis
The Dying Wish	Courttia Newland
The Grey Man	Andy McNab
I Am a Dalek	Gareth Roberts
I Love Football	Hunter Davies
The Name You Once Gave Me	Mike Phillips
The Poison in the Blood	Tom Holland
Winner Takes All	John Francome

**Look out for more titles in the *Quick* Reads
series in 2007.**

www.worldbookday.com

Have you enjoyed reading this
Quick Reads **book?**

Would you like to read more?

Or learn how to write fantastically?

If so, you might like to attend a course to
develop your skills.

Courses are **free** and available in your local area.

If you'd like to find out more,
phone **0800 100 900.**

You can also ask for a **free video or DVD** showing
other people who have been on our courses and
the changes they have made in their lives.

Don't get by – get on.

Don't get by get on 0800 100 900

FIRST CHOICE BOOKS

If you enjoyed this book, you'll find more great reads on www.firstchoicebooks.org.uk. First Choice Books allows you to search by type of book, author and title. So, whether you're looking for romance, sport, humour – or whatever turns you on – you'll be able to find other books you'll enjoy.

You can also borrow books from your local library. If you tell them what you've enjoyed, they can recommend other good reads they think you will like.

First Choice is part of The Vital Link, promoting reading for pleasure. To find out more about the Vital Link visit www.vitallink.org.uk

RaW

Find out what the BBC's RaW (Reading and Writing) campaign has to offer at www.bbc.co.uk/raw

NEW ISLAND

New Island publishers have produced four series of books in its Open Door series – brilliant short novels for adults from the cream of Irish writers. Visit www.newisland.ie and go to the Open Door section.

SANDSTONE PRESS

In the Sandstone Vista Series, Sandstone Press Ltd publish quality contemporary fiction and non-fiction books. The full list can be found at their website www.sandstonepress.com.

Quick Reads

Don't Make Me Laugh by Patrick Augustus

The X Press

It's not funny. Leo and Trevor are twins, but they hate each other's guts. Leo says his brother got off with his woman. Trevor reckons it was the other way round. Only Mum can stop them ripping each other to bits. But HER big secret is that one of them has to die.

Quick Reads

Someone Like Me by Tom Holt

Orbit

When the hunter becomes the prey . . .

In a world torn apart by hatred and fear, only the strongest survive.

Nobody knows where they came from. Nobody knows what they want. The creatures are killing humans for meat and nobody, it seems, can stop them.

Now one man – a hunter by trade – has trapped one of the creatures. Under the ground they face each other. Only one of them will get out alive.

Quick Reads

Screw It, Let's Do It by Richard Branson

Virgin

Learn the secrets of a global icon.

Throughout my life I have strived for success –
as a businessman, in my adventures, as an
author and a proud father and husband. I want
to share the many truths I've learned along the
road to success which have helped me to be the
best I can. They include:

Have faith in yourself
Believe that anything can be done
Don't let other people put you off
Never give up

Learn these and other simple truths, and I hope
you will be inspired to get the most out of your
life and to achieve your goals. People will try to
talk you out of ideas and say, 'It can't be done,'
but if you have faith in yourself you'll find you
can achieve almost anything.

Quick Reads

Blackwater by Conn Iggulden

HarperCollins

Blackwater is a cold, dark thriller with a twist.

Davy has always lived in the shadow of his older brother, who will stop at nothing to protect himself and his family. But when Denis Tanter comes into Davey's life, how far will they go to get him out of trouble?

How far can you go before you're in too deep?

Quick Reads

Chickenfeed by Minette Walters

Pan Books

This book is based on the true story of the 'chicken farm murder', which took place at Blackness, Crowborough, East Sussex in December 1924.

Norman Thorne was found guilty of the murder of Elsie Cameron, but even at the time of his execution there were doubts about his conviction. Still swearing his innocence, Norman Thorne was hanged on 22 April 1925.

Minette Walters brings a thrilling story to life in this gripping new novel.